MW00585433

The Mystery of the Golden Reindeer

THREE COUSINS DETECTIVE CLUB®

The Mystery of the Golden Reindeer

Elspeth Campbell Murphy

Illustrated by Joe Nordstrom

BETHANY HOUSE PUBLISHERS
MINNEAPOLIS, MINNESOTA 55438

The Mystery of the Golden Reindeer
Copyright © 2000
Elspeth Campbell Murphy

Cover and story illustrations by Joe Nordstrom
Cover design by Lookout Design Group, Inc.

THREE COUSINS DETECTIVE CLUB® and TCDC® are
registered trademarks of Elspeth Campbell Murphy.

Scripture quotation is from the *Bible in Today's English Version* (*Good
News Bible*). Copyright © American Bible Society 1966, 1971, 1976,
1992

All rights reserved. No part of this publication may be reproduced,
stored in a retrieval system, or transmitted in any form or by any
means—electronic, mechanical, photocopying, recording, or
otherwise—without the prior written permission of the publisher and
copyright owners.

Published by Bethany House Publishers
A Ministry of Bethany Fellowship International
11400 Hampshire Avenue South
Bloomington, Minnesota 55438
www.bethanyhouse.com

Printed in the United States of America by
Bethany Press International, Bloomington, Minnesota 55438

Library of Congress Cataloging-in-Publication Data

Murphy, Elspeth Campbell.
    The mystery of the golden reindeer / by Elspeth Campbell
Murphy ;
illustrated by Joe Nordstrom.
        p. cm. — (Three Cousins Detective Club ; 30)
    Summary: At Christmas time the three cousins hear a story about
a mysterious golden reindeer and wonder if they will be the ones to
find it.
    ISBN 0–7642–2138–8 (pbk.)
    [1. Christmas—Fiction. 2. Cousins—Fiction. 3. Mystery and
detective stories.] I. Nordstrom, Joe, ill. II. Title.
PZ7.M95316 Mybh   2000
    [Fic]—dc21

                                                    00–010530

ELSPETH CAMPBELL MURPHY has been a familiar name in Christian publishing for over twenty years, with more than one hundred books to her credit and sales approaching six million worldwide. She is the author of the bestselling series *David and I Talk to God* and *The Kids From Apple Street Church,* as well as the 1990 Gold Medallion winner *Do You See Me, God?,* and two books of prayer meditations for teachers, *Chalkdust* and *Recess.* A graduate of Trinity College and Moody Bible Institute, Elspeth and her husband, Mike, make their home in Chicago, where she writes full time.

Contents

What you get from wisdom
is better than the finest gold.

Proverbs 8:19

1

Christmas Shopping

"*B*ut that's exactly the problem with Christmas shopping," said Titus McKay. "It always sounds like more fun than it really is."

His cousins Timothy Dawson and Sarah-Jane Cooper did not look convinced.

They were visiting Titus in the city. And Titus could tell that the idea of a big, downtown department store at Christmastime sounded like *lots* of fun to them.

Titus's mother had given them the choice of staying home or going with her. But whatever they chose, the three of them had to stay together.

"OK. Let's vote on it," said Titus. "All those who want to stay home and have a wonderful, relaxing time with popcorn and videos, raise your hands."

Titus raised his own hand.

It was the only one in the air.

"OK," said Titus with a heavy sigh. "All those who want to clomp around a noisy, crowded department store, getting bored out of your minds, raise your hands."

Sarah-Jane and Timothy waved their hands in the air.

Sarah-Jane loved to shop, so of course she wanted to go.

Timothy hate to shop, but he loved art. And the Christmas decorations were always fabulous.

Titus knew when he was licked.

"All right," he said darkly. "We'll go Christmas shopping. But my mother also said she wants to look at *furniture*! So don't say you weren't *warned*!"

He said this in such a scary voice that Timothy and Sarah-Jane burst out laughing.

Titus found himself laughing along with them.

It was just Christmas shopping, after all.

What could possibly go wrong?

2

The Spectacular Scarf

Now that he was outvoted, Titus decided to make the best of it.

After all, Timothy and Sarah-Jane didn't live in the city. Going to Hill's Department Store was a special treat for them. Titus had been going to Hill's ever since he was a baby in a stroller. He knew his way around pretty well, and he could be a good host.

In honor of the occasion, he even decided to wear his new scarf. His grandaunt Barbara had made it especially for him. It was *very* long. Black and white. With a bold zigzag pattern. Titus had never seen another scarf quite like it. And he loved his the first moment he saw it.

So did Timothy and Sarah-Jane.

"Wow!" said Timothy. "Neat-O scarf, Ti!"

"So cool!" agreed Sarah-Jane.

Titus laughed. "It makes it easy to pick me out in a crowd."

Sarah-Jane frowned. "Why would we have to pick you out in a crowd?"

"Yeah," said Timothy. "You know the rule."

It was the rule in all three families. Sometimes the cousins were allowed to go off by themselves. But they couldn't go off alone. It had to be the three of them.

"It was just an expression," said Titus, loudly enough for his mother to hear. "I *know* we have to stick together. And we always do. That's because we're *such* good kids. *Other* kids might run all over the place and get into trouble in a department store. But not us. No, sir. We can go off to the toy department by ourselves, and no one ever has to worry about us."

From the other room his mother said, "I thought you wanted to look at furniture with me."

"Hmmm," Titus replied. "I don't know, Mom. Toys. Furniture. Toys. Furniture. It's so hard to decide!"

"Well," said his mother. "We'll see. It depends on how crowded the store is. If it's not too bad, maybe you can be on your own for a little while."

The cousins grinned so hard Titus thought they must look like chimpanzees. They clapped their hands without actually letting their hands touch. They were somehow afraid that if they made a lot of noise, Titus's mother would change her mind. Grown-ups could be unpredictable that way.

"Well, what are we waiting for?" asked Titus, tossing his spectacular scarf over his shoulder. "Let's go!"

3

A Surprise in the Toy Department

*I*t was early, and the store wasn't too crowded. So Mrs. McKay agreed the cousins could go by themselves to look at toys.

They picked a time to meet at the store restaurant on the top floor. Whoever got there first would hold a place in line.

And it could be a very long line. The restaurant was a popular place because of the *huge* Christmas tree in the center of the room. It was a favorite tradition to eat under the tree at Hill's.

"Stay together," said Mrs. McKay as she headed off.

"Always," said the cousins.

There were three ways to get up to the toy department on the fourth floor.

You could take the escalator.

You could take the regular elevator.

Or you could take the new, all-glass elevator at the center of the store.

It wasn't much of a decision.

The cousins headed to the glass elevator without even stopping to talk about it.

The glass elevator was not a good idea if you were afraid of heights. But the cousins weren't. In fact, they decided to ride all the way to the top floor and then back down to toys.

It was a breathtaking ride. Up, up, up, gliding past the floors and looking out at the gorgeous decorations. Mostly reindeer. All golden and shiny. And because of the way they were hung up, the golden reindeer seemed to be leaping and flying through the air.

If the cousins thought the elevator ride was fabulous, the toy department was even better.

There was another long line here, too. It was for the little kids to see Santa.

But there was stuff for older kids, too.

Hill's Department Store always set out some sample toys that you could actually play with to see if you liked them.

And every year there was a model train with a whole toy village around it, which was just for looking at.

Sarah-Jane just couldn't get enough of the train. Titus figured she was probably making up stories about all the imaginary people who lived in the village.

It would have been easy to lose track of time. But Titus kept an eye on his watch so they wouldn't be late to the restaurant.

He was just about to tell Timothy and Sarah-Jane they had to go, when the Christmas carols stopped. And there came an announcement over the loudspeaker:

"Attention. May we have your attention, please? We have a report of a lost child, last seen in the toy department. Her name is Patience. She's four years old. She has red hair. And she is wearing a blue coat. If you have any information, please report it immediately. Thank you."

Timothy, Titus, and Sarah-Jane stared at one another in astonishment.

It *couldn't* be! *Could* it?

But before they could say a word, someone said to them, "HEY, YOU GUYS! WHERE DID YOU GET TO? I'VE BEEN LOOKING ALL OVER FOR YOU!"

4

Lost and Found

*T*he cousins whirled around to see a little girl in a blue coat, whose hair was the exact same shade of red as Sarah-Jane's. She stood with her hands on her hips, looking at them as if she were the teacher and they were a misbehaving class.

"Patience!" gasped Sarah-Jane. "It's *you!* Are you lost?"

Patience shrugged. "No. I'm right here. I don't know *where* Nonny went to."

Nonny, the cousins knew, was Patience's grandmother. Her name was Patience, too. And the cousins called her Aunt Patience, even though she wasn't really their aunt. She was their grandmother's cousin. Little Patience was their third cousin. They had met her only a couple of times. And both times had been . . . well . . . interesting.

"Nonny!" cried Timothy suddenly. "She must be worried sick! We have to find her."

"I *told* you she was lost," said Patience.

Without another word, Titus snatched Patience by the hand and dragged her toward the nearest checkout counter. Timothy and Sarah-Jane scurried along behind.

"Excuse us! Excuse us!" said Titus to the crowds around them. "Coming through! Coming through! We found the little lost girl!"

As soon as people heard that, they stepped aside.

"You didn't find *me*!" Patience protested. "I finded *you*!"

Titus wisely ignored that and explained to the clerk that they had found the little lost girl.

The clerk immediately picked up the phone and said to Titus, "What's her mother's name?"

"She's with her grandmother," said Titus. "Her name is . . ." Suddenly his mind went blank. "Patience, what's your grandmother's name?"

"Nonny," said Patience.

"No, no, I mean her last name."

"Grandmothers don't have last names," said Patience, sounding amazed that he didn't know that.

"It's North!" said Sarah-Jane suddenly. "The same as little Patience."

So the clerk made the call. And then the announcement came over the loudspeaker:

"Attention! Attention! May we have your attention, please? Will Mrs. North please report to the counter nearest the model train in the toy department? We have your granddaughter. To repeat, the missing little girl has been found. She's waiting by the model train in the toy department. Thank you."

The crowd around them burst into applause.

And seconds later, Nonny came rushing toward them. Her face was pale, and her hand was clasped over her chest.

"Oh, Patience! What a fright you gave me! I've been looking all over for you!" she cried.

Nonny said to the people around her, "I just turned around for a second and she was gone!" They nodded kindly and said the same thing had once happened to them.

Nonny turned back to Patience. "What a naughty thing to do! To run off and hide like that!"

"But I didn't!" cried Patience indignantly, as if she had never done anything naughty in her whole entire life. In fact—as the cousins well knew—hiding was her specialty.

"I was just following *those* guys!" she said, pointing at the cousins. "But then *they* got lost, and I finded them!"

"Wait a minute," muttered Timothy. "How did this get to be *our* fault?"

Nonny noticed the cousins for the first time. "Titus! Sarah-Jane! Timothy! What a lovely surprise! What are you doing here? But you live in the city, don't you, Titus? Patience and I just took the train in for the day. Her parents have the flu, so I brought her in to see Santa. Now we're headed upstairs to eat under the tree."

"That's where we're going, too," said Titus. "We're meeting my mom there, right now."

"So we can all go together," said Sarah-Jane happily.

Hanging out with Patience was not Titus's idea of a good time. But it was just lunch. What could possibly go wrong?

5

Trouble

"*I*'m scared of es-calligators," announced Patience importantly as they walked along.

"Alligators?" said Timothy. "Who isn't scared of alligators? You're supposed to be scared of them."

"Although I think crocodiles might actually be more dangerous," said Titus, who knew a lot about animals.

"NO! NO! NO!" cried Patience. "Not *real* alligators, silly! That other thing!"

"Well, that narrows it down," said Titus. "What other thing?"

Patience sighed. "You know! The thing with steps on it."

Titus glanced over at Nonny, who was laughing to herself. There was something they weren't getting here.

"*Escalators!*" cried Sarah-Jane suddenly.

"You're scared of *escalators*!"

"Very good, Sarah-Jane!" said Nonny. "I wondered if you would figure that one out."

Es-calligators! thought Titus. Patience certainly had her own way of putting things.

"I was scared of escalators, too, when I was little," he found himself admitting. It surprised him to have something in common with Patience, of all people.

"A lot of small children are," said Nonny. "They have trouble catching the first step. By the way, I love your scarf, Titus."

"Thank you," said Titus. "My grandaunt Barbara made it for me."

So they took the elevator. The cousins nicely let Patience push the button for the seventh floor, even though it took her longer to find it.

When they got to the restaurant, Titus's mother was already there, holding a place in line.

She was delighted to see Nonny again. And to meet little Patience for the first time.

But Titus could tell right away that something was wrong. He was in some kind of trouble. But what? Even with finding Patience, they still got to the restaurant right on time.

He knew his mother wouldn't embarrass

him by yelling at him in front of Nonny. But he almost wished she would. The suspense was killing him.

When his mother heard about Patience wandering off, she finally said, "Aha! That's just what I wanted to talk to Titus about! I thought you promised me that you would stay with your cousins."

Titus blinked at her. "But I did. I was with them the whole time."

His mother sighed. "Honey, I *saw* you. Not ten minutes ago. You were going down the escalator. All by yourself. You promised me that you would stay with Timothy and Sarah-Jane."

"But he did, Aunt Jane!" exclaimed Timothy.

"Ti was with us the whole time!" agreed Sarah-Jane.

They were nodding so hard Titus thought their heads might fall off. That was nice of them.

"Well, kiddo," said his mother. "I guess I owe you an apology."

Titus heaved a deep sigh and shook his head. "It's a sad, sad day when your own mother doesn't recognize you."

"It's just that—I could have *sworn* I saw you," said his mother.

Patience, who had been quiet for a change, spoke up. Matter-of-factly she said, "Oh, that wasn't the *real* Titus. That was the other Titus."

6

Tall Tales

*N*onny and Titus's mother laughed gently at this. And the cousins rolled their eyes.

But before anyone could ask Patience what she was talking about, the host told them their table was ready.

Everyone gasped when they saw the tree. Like the rest of the store, it was decorated with golden reindeer.

"Santa Claus has reindeer," said Patience, as if she had new information for everybody.

"Did you see Santa?" Titus's mother asked her.

"Yes," replied Patience. "He asked me if I'd been a good girl all year."

The cousins glanced at one another with raised eyebrows. They'd been with Patience a couple of times this past year. Based on what they'd seen, she was on pretty shaky ground.

"Just out of curiosity," said Titus. "What did you tell him?"

Patience grinned. "I told him, 'GOT THAT RIGHT!'"

Several tables turned around to look.

"Shhh!" said Nonny. "Use your indoor voice, please."

The cousins glanced at one another again. From what they knew of Patience, she had only two voices. Loud. And louder.

"THERE HE GOES AGAIN!" cried Patience, bouncing up and down in her chair.

"Patience, please!" said Nonny.

"There *who* goes again?" asked Titus's mother.

"The other Titus!" said Patience, as if this was perfectly obvious. "He's outside the restaurant. He just got on the es-calligator!"

"The what?" asked Titus's mother.

"Escalator," said Sarah-Jane, turning around to look. "I don't see anything."

Neither did anyone else.

"Are you sure this isn't like Amy?" Nonny asked Patience.

"Who's Amy?" asked Sarah-Jane.

"Patience has a little friend that only she can see," explained Nonny. "Amy is always in trouble."

Titus's mother nodded. "An imaginary playmate. Titus had a friend named Sam. Sam got blamed for everything."

Timothy and Sarah-Jane laughed. Titus groaned. Something else he had in common with Patience. How weird was that?

And what was all this stuff about the other Titus?

Patience was known for her "tall tales." The grown-ups said it wasn't *lying* at her age. She just had a lot of imagination.

But that was the thing about Patience. You couldn't tell if she was making up some wild story. Or if she was telling you the truth in her own weird little way.

She once told Titus, Timothy, and Sarah-Jane that she had made some angels dance.

Another time she told them that a penguin had put a surprise in her flower girl basket.

Tall tales.

The problem was, both those stories had turned out to be true.

So what was all this about the other Titus?

Was there really someone out there who looked exactly like him?

Was Patience imagining things?

Was his mother?

Titus couldn't explain it. But it made him feel very uneasy.

Very uneasy, indeed.

7

Lunch Under the Christmas Tree

"*S*o—did you have a good time looking at toys?" asked Titus's mother over lunch.

"Yes, thank you," said Titus. "Did you have a good time looking at furniture?"

"Actually, I didn't get there yet," said his mother. "I bought a couple of presents. And then I came up here early to get in line."

"What kind of furniture are you looking for?" asked Nonny.

Mrs. McKay launched into a detailed description, with Nonny hanging on every word. Titus remembered that Nonny was an expert about houses and furniture.

Titus gazed at the glorious Christmas tree and just kind of let the conversation flow over him. He wasn't totally zoned out. But he wasn't totally tuned in, either.

31

Then he heard his mother say, "Aunt Patience, I would just *love* to get your advice! Maybe after lunch, we could all go up to the furniture department together."

"Oh, I'd enjoy that!" said Nonny.

Titus glanced at his mother and Nonny. He could tell by the looks on their faces that this visit to the furniture department could last until the end of time.

Titus felt Timothy kick him under the table. It meant, "*Do* something!"

"Mom," Titus said, "while you're doing that, can we go look at the store windows?"

The minute the words were out of his mouth, he knew they were a mistake.

"I WANT TO LOOK AT THE WINDOWS, TOO! MAKE THEM TAKE ME!"

"Of course they will, sweetie," said Titus's mother. "As long as it's OK with Nonny."

Nonny hesitated. She had already lost Patience once today.

"It will be okay, Aunt Patience," said Sarah-Jane. "Patience only ran off because she saw us in the toy department and she wanted to play with us. So if she gets to be with us, there's no reason for her to run off. She'll be good. Won't you, Patience?"

Titus knew Sarah-Jane would feel sorry for

any little kid who had to look at furniture. But this was *Patience* they were talking about. He tried to kick Sarah-Jane under the table. But he missed and kicked Timothy instead, which did no good at all.

Patience nodded her little head and said, "I'll be good, Nonny."

She sounded so serious that even Titus believed her.

How had this happened?

It was wonderful that his mother trusted them enough to let them go off on their own again. But with *Patience*? Maybe Nonny would say no.

"OK," said Nonny. "But hold Sarah-Jane's hand, and do what she tells you."

Again Patience nodded.

Titus reminded himself of what he had told himself that morning. It was only Christmas shopping. What could possibly go wrong?

Ha!

8

Empty Boxes

*T*hey hadn't gone very far when Sarah-Jane said, "Wait. I have to stop at the rest room." Timothy had to stop, too. So that left Titus to watch Patience. They sat down on a bench near the rest rooms to wait for the others.

Patience pointed to a nearby display of a Christmas tree with gaily wrapped boxes underneath.

"Who are those presents for?" she asked.

"No one," said Titus.

"Does that mean anybody can open them?" asked Patience, sounding a little too interested.

"No! It means they're not presents at all."

"They look like presents."

"But they're not. They're just empty boxes wrapped up to look like presents."

"Why?"

"Why what?"

35

"Why did they wrap up empty boxes?"

"Just for decoration."

"Why?"

"To make the store look pretty for Christmas. You can see displays like that all over the place."

Patience was quiet for a moment. Then she said, "Christmas is Jesus' birthday."

"Yes, I know," said Titus, glad for a change of subject.

Patience nodded. "So maybe those are His presents. Maybe we should open them for Him."

"Patience!"

"What?"

"Don't even think about it. I mean it. You leave those boxes alone."

"OK."

Titus sighed. Another weird little conversation with Patience.

And if the conversation with Patience wasn't weird enough, things suddenly got weirder.

9

The Strange Message

A very crabby-looking teenage boy came up to Titus and said, "There you are! I've been looking all over for you. Now listen up. I haven't got all day. The message is: Happy Birthday. The golden reindeer. Dish towels. Christmas tree."

Titus blinked at him. "What?"

"Just what I said."

"But what are you talking about?"

"Look, pal. Don't play dumb. You knew someone was going to meet you here today at Hill's. That's me, OK? I didn't make up the message. I was just paid to deliver it. That's what I did. And now I'm out of here."

"Wait, I don't understand . . ." began Titus.

But it was too late.

The boy got on an elevator and was gone.

"Who was that?" asked Timothy as he and Sarah-Jane came back from the rest rooms.

"I have no idea," said Titus.

"What did he want?" asked Sarah-Jane.

"He told Titus not to be dumb," said Patience.

Titus sighed. "He told me not to *play* dumb when I said I didn't understand the message."

"Message? What message?" asked Timothy.

"It was so weird," said Titus. "He said he had a message for me. He said he'd been looking all over for me and that the message wasn't from him. He'd just been paid to deliver it. And that I knew someone would be meeting me here today at the department store."

"What did the message say?" asked Sarah-Jane.

Before Titus could reply, Patience said, "That boy said, 'Now, listen up. I haven't got all day. The message is: Happy Birthday. The golden reindeer. Dish towels. Christmas tree.'"

Timothy and Sarah-Jane burst out laughing.

"No, really, Ti," said Timothy. "What did the guy say?"

"That's it," said Titus. "Word for word."

Timothy and Sarah-Jane stared at him.

"You're kidding, right?" said Timothy.

"I wish I were," said Titus.

Sarah-Jane said, "So some guy just came up to you and said—what? 'Happy Birthday. The golden reindeer. Dish towels. Christmas tree'?"

"That's right," said Titus.

Timothy and Sarah-Jane just kept staring at him.

Titus sighed and shook his head. It was a sad, sad day when something really weird happened and the only person who could back up your story was Patience.

"That guy must have been crazy," said Timothy at last.

"He didn't seem crazy," said Titus. "He just seemed annoyed that it had been so hard to find me."

He stopped suddenly as a new thought struck him.

"What? What is it?" asked Sarah-Jane.

Titus said slowly, "Maybe the guy wasn't looking for *me* at all. Maybe that's why I didn't understand the message. Maybe it was meant for someone else."

"Who?" asked Timothy.

"Someone who looks just like me?" suggested Titus.

The three of them looked at Patience with

new respect. Maybe her tall tale about the "other Titus" wasn't so ridiculous after all. . . .

Patience looked back at them and said, "I HAVE TO GO POTTY!"

10

The T.C.D.C.

Sarah-Jane sighed. "Why didn't you tell me that a few minutes ago?"

"I didn't know I had to go then," said Patience.

It was pretty hard to argue with that.

"OK," Sarah-Jane said to the boys. "You guys wait here. We'll be right back."

"So what do you think we ought to do?" Timothy said.

Titus knew right away what he was talking about. The three cousins were good at solving mysteries. They even had a club called the T.C.D.C. It stood for the Three Cousins Detective Club.

"Well," said Titus. "I guess we could look for this 'other Titus.' That's assuming he really does exist. We could give him the message and ask him what it means."

"Or," said Timothy, "while we're looking for this guy, we could try to figure out the message ourselves."

"Golden reindeer," said Titus thoughtfully. "There are only about a gazillion of them in the store."

"The same for Christmas trees," agreed Timothy. "And Happy Birthday. What does that mean? I mean, I know what it *means*, but what does it mean in the message?"

"And dish towels," said Titus. "Dish towels!"

Just then Sarah-Jane and Patience came back.

"HEY, YOU GUYS!" Patience cried, as if she hadn't seen them for years.

"Hey, Patience," said Timothy and Titus together.

Detective work still sounded like a good idea, but it was going to be harder with you-know-who around.

"Are we going to see the windows now?" said Patience.

"Yes," said Titus. "We're going to see the windows now. But I think we'll take a little side trip first."

Timothy and Sarah-Jane looked at him in surprise.

"Where are we going, Ti?" they asked.

They looked at him as if he was out of his mind when Titus said, "Kitchen stuff."

11

The Es-calligator

"*Kitchen stuff!*" exclaimed Timothy. "What are you—nuts? That's even more boring than furniture!"

"Tell me about it!" agreed Titus. "But it's the only part of the message we can do anything about. We don't know whose birthday it is. We don't know which reindeer to look at. Or which Christmas tree. But at least we know where the dish towels are. Maybe there's some kind of clue there."

Timothy and Sarah-Jane shrugged. It was a place to start, anyway.

Patience didn't complain. She just seemed happy to be wherever the big kids were.

But when Sarah-Jane took her hand and headed toward the elevators, Patience pulled back. "No, no, no! Not the elevator. I want to ride the es-calligator!"

"Are you sure?" Titus asked her. "I thought you were scared of es-calligators. I mean, escalators."

Patience didn't answer. And Titus knew she was still scared. But she wanted to try it anyway. What a kid.

"OK," said Sarah-Jane. "But if you decide not to, that's all right, too."

Unfortunately, they had to go down to get to the kitchen department. And going down the escalator was scarier than going up.

At the top of the escalator, Patience froze. All those steps, coming out of nowhere. But she wouldn't give up and go on the elevator, either.

"Great," muttered Timothy. "We're going to be here forever."

Some people came up behind them and were getting impatient. So Timothy and Titus each took one of her hands.

"On the count of three," said Titus. "One. Two. Three."

Then they lifted Patience up and put her on the top step, squeezing in beside her, with Sarah-Jane on the step behind.

"I DID IT!" cried Patience, grinning nervously as they glided down.

"Yes, you did," said Titus.

Patience kept at it—down and up, down and up— until she was able to get on just by holding onto Sarah-Jane with one hand and the railing with the other.

"Wait till I tell Nonny I rided the es-calligator!" said Patience. She said it with such delight that Titus couldn't help smiling.

He was paying so much attention to Patience that he almost missed the boy going past them on the up escalator.

A boy with dark hair and glasses. A boy with a long black-and-white scarf. A boy who looked exactly like him.

At the same moment, the boy saw Titus, and his mouth dropped open.

Titus knew how he felt. It was like looking in a mirror.

What could they do?

Desperately, Titus called out to him as the boy rode up and they rode down. "Meet us in kitchen stuff!"

But whether the boy heard him or not, Titus couldn't tell.

12

The Other Titus

"*D*id you *see* that?" squeaked Timothy as they stepped off the escalator into the kitchen department. "That guy looked *exactly* like Ti! *Exactly!*"

"I *know*!" gasped Sarah-Jane. "I couldn't believe my eyes!"

Patience just shrugged. "I seed him before. He's the other Titus."

The cousins glanced at one another.

The other Titus.

So Patience had been right.

Again.

"That must be who my mom saw," said Titus. "That's why she thought I wasn't with you guys."

But they didn't have time to talk about it, because suddenly the other Titus was right there behind them.

Close up, they could tell he was taller than Titus and maybe a few years older. And his long black-and-white scarf had checks, not zig-zags. But other than that, the resemblance to Titus was amazing.

"Uh—hi," said the boy a little uncertainly. "I thought I heard you say to meet you in kitchen stuff. That seemed kind of weird, but I guess I was right."

"Yes!" said Titus. "Thank goodness you heard me! I don't know if we could have found you again otherwise. In fact, if our little cousin hadn't wanted to try the es-calligator, we might not have seen you at all."

"The what?" asked the boy.

Titus felt his face grow hot. "I mean, the *escalator.*" (Would he ever remember to say it the right way again? How embarrassing!)

"So anyway," he went on quickly. "Patience kept talking about this 'other Titus,' someone who looks like me. I'm Titus, by the way.

"Then this guy came up to me and gave me a weird message that I didn't understand at all. So I figured maybe the message was meant for you."

"Yes! Yes!" cried the boy. "That's why I'm here! I got this strange phone call saying if I wanted to get something back that belongs to my family, I should come to the department store. Someone would contact me and tell me where the thing is.

"The caller told me the messenger would know what I look like. You know—dark hair, glasses. But he also told me to wear something noticeable. So I told him I would be wearing a long black-and-white scarf.

"I've been wandering all over, waiting for someone to come up to me. But—what are we doing in kitchen stuff?"

"It's because of the message," explained Timothy. "It said: 'Happy Birthday. The golden reindeer. Christmas tree. Dish towels.'

We figured dish towels was the only clue we understood. So we thought we'd come check it out—because of being the T.C.D.C., I mean."

"The what?" asked the boy. "What's a 'teesy-deesy'?"

"It's letters," explained Sarah-Jane. "Capital T. Capital C. Capital D. Capital C. It stands for the Three Cousins Detective Club."

"Oh," said the boy, as if he wasn't at all sure what to make of people who said things like *escalligator* and *teesy-deesy.*

"So what does the message mean?" asked Sarah-Jane. "We're dying of curiosity."

But the boy (who they learned was named Henry) just shook his head in frustration. "I have no idea!"

No one quite knew what to say next. And things got kind of quiet. It occurred to Titus that they hadn't heard from Patience in a while.

But when he turned to check on her, Patience was gone.

13

Clues

*T*itus felt his whole body flood with panic.

"Patience! *Patience!*" he cried.

"What?"

The unusually quiet little voice sounded as if it was only a few feet away.

Titus looked around desperately.

"Patience, where are you?"

"Nowhere."

"Patience, I mean it!"

Patience must have believed him, because she crawled out from behind a Christmas tree at the end of the aisle.

Sarah-Jane gasped. "Patience! Were you *hiding*? After you promised to be a good girl?"

Patience shook her head wildly. "No, no, no! I was *not* hiding."

"Then what were you doing down there?" asked Timothy.

Patience didn't answer. She just looked down guiltily.

"*I* know what you were doing down there!" said Titus. "You were opening boxes, weren't you?"

Again Patience shook her head. "No, no, no! I didn't open any."

"Then what were you doing?" asked Titus. "Shaking them to see if there was anything inside?"

Patience didn't answer, and he knew he had hit the nail on the head.

"Patience, what did I tell you about those boxes upstairs? I said they were just for decoration, didn't I? I said they were empty."

"You said *those* boxes were empty," said Patience. "You didn't say *these* boxes were empty."

"Aurgggh!" said Titus. "They're *all* empty. All the decoration-boxes in the whole entire store are empty. Now, get out of there before you get us all in trouble."

"*This* box isn't empty," said Patience, shaking the box in her hand. "See? It rattles."

The cousins and Henry stared at the box. It seemed to strike them all at once.

Patience was sitting under a *Christmas tree.*

The Christmas tree was at the end of the aisle by the *dish towels.*

Titus took the decorated package from Patience and looked at it closely.

The wrapping paper was the same color as the other packages, so the box sort of blended in.

But it was different, too.

This box wasn't wrapped in Christmas paper.

You had to look closely to see the difference.

But this paper definitely said *Happy Birthday.*

14

The Golden Reindeer

"*I*t's all the clues in the weird message!" said Timothy. " 'Happy Birthday. The golden reindeer. Christmas tree. Dish towels.' Well, it's everything except the golden reindeer, that is."

He looked up at the leaping reindeer decorations around the store. "I wonder what that part of the message means?"

"I know what it means," said Henry. "The golden reindeer doesn't mean the store decorations. The golden reindeer is the thing that belongs to my family. The thing that was stolen and that I came to get back."

"Do you think the golden reindeer is in the box?" asked Sarah-Jane.

"Only one way to find out," said Titus, handing the box to Henry.

Very, very carefully, Henry began to unwrap the package. He explained that if they were wrong, he wanted to put the package back without making a mess.

It made perfect sense. But it was still nerve-wracking to wait.

Patience started to protest that she should be the one to open it. But Titus gave her a warning glance. And she seemed to realize that she shouldn't push her luck.

They were not wrong about the package.

Henry opened the box and pulled out a beautiful necklace. It was just a simple golden chain. And dangling from the chain was a perfect little reindeer that seemed to leap for Christmas joy.

Everyone gasped. Even Timothy and Titus, who didn't care much about jewelry.

"It was my grandmother's," said Henry softly. "And it was stolen many years ago. I guess someone wanted to return it."

"Without anyone finding out who took it," said Timothy.

"So he hid it in a busy department store," said Sarah-Jane. "And told you where to find it. I guess he thought he was putting it in a safe place."

"But nothing is safe from Patience," said Titus.

Patience nodded happily. "GOT THAT RIGHT!"

15

Christmas Windows

"*I* don't know how to thank you guys," said Henry.

Timothy and Sarah-Jane started to say, "No problem. Forget about it. We were glad to help."

But Titus said, "Well, actually. There *is* something you can do for me."

"Name it," said Henry.

"Come with us to the furniture department," said Titus.

Mrs. McKay's mouth dropped open when she saw Titus and Henry together.

She said to Titus, "It's not that I didn't *believe* you before, but now . . ."

"But now you know that I was falsely accused," said Titus. "And I am really the perfect son who never, ever does anything wrong."

"Uh, well . . ." said his mother.

"And speaking of perfect children," said Nonny. "How was my little Patience? How did you like the windows?"

"Uh . . . we didn't get there yet," said Titus.

Nonny and his mother looked at him in surprise. But before he could explain, someone said:

"AND, AND, YOU KNOW WHAT? I FINDED THE GOLDEN REINDEER!"

Nonny smiled at her. "Now, Patience. Is this another one of your tall tales?"

"Noooo," said Titus. "Actually it isn't."

It took a while—quite a while—to explain about the mysterious message and the hidden treasure and why they hadn't even gotten to see the windows yet.

"AND, AND—YOU KNOW WHAT? I RIDED THE ES—THE ES . . ."

"The es-ca-la-tor," said Titus.

"The es-ca-la-tor," said Patience.

Henry thanked them again for their help and happily took the golden reindeer home.

Nonny and Mrs. McKay went with the cousins and Patience to see the gorgeous store windows.

The theme was "The Twelve Days of Christmas."

Timothy, Titus, and Sarah-Jane took turns

reading aloud the captions over the displays:

Twelve ladies dancing.
Eleven lords a-leaping.
Ten drummers drumming.
Nine pipers piping.
Eight maids a-milking.
Seven swans a-swimming.
Six geese a-laying.
Five golden rings.
Four calling birds.
Three French hens.
Two turtle doves.
And a partridge in a pear tree.

Patience loved the colors and the moving figures. But she kept asking why the person in the story got such dumb presents. No one had a good answer for that. So Patience kept asking. And it got pretty boring.

But then something good happened.

Someone nudged Titus in the back. He turned around to see who it was and came face-to-face with a horse he knew.

It was a police horse named Sparky. And riding him was Officer Simons. Titus and his cousins had met them a couple of months ago at the Blessing of the Animals.

"THAT HORSE THINKS HE'S SANTA CLAUS!" cried Patience.

"What in the world are you talking about now?" Titus asked her.

Then he saw that, sure enough, Sparky was wearing a Santa Claus hat.

Patience slipped her hand into Titus's. "Can we pet him?" she asked.

"Sparky loves the attention," said Officer Simons.

Titus was impressed to see that Patience was not the least bit afraid of Sparky. And even more amazing—Sparky was not the least bit afraid of Patience.

"So are you enjoying your Christmas shopping?" Officer Simons asked them.

"You know how it is with Christmas shopping," Titus replied. "It's always so much better than you think it's going to be."

The End